P9-DUE-154

Jamestown:
The First English Colony

Mitchell Lane
PUBLISHERS

P.O. Box 196 • Hockessin, Delaware 19707

Titles in the Series

Georgia: The Debtors Colony

**Holidays and Celebrations
in Colonial America**

Jamestown: The First English Colony

**The Massachusetts Bay Colony:
The Puritans Arrive from England**

**New Netherland: The Dutch
Settle the Hudson Valley**

**Pennsylvania: William Penn and
the City of Brotherly Love**

**The Plymouth Colony: The Pilgrims
Settle in New England**

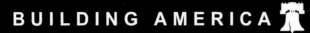

Jamestown:
The First English Colony

Susan Harkins and William H. Harkins

Printing   2   3   4   5   6   7   8   9

Library of Congress Cataloging-in-Publication Data
Harkins, Susan Sales.
        Jamestown: the first English colony/by Susan and William Harkins.
                p. cm.—(Building America.)
        Includes bibliographical references and index.
        ISBN 1-58415-458-6 (library bound)
        1. Jamestown (Va.)—History—17th century—Juvenile literature. 2. Frontier and
pioneer life—Virginia—Jamestown—Juvenile literature. 3. Virginia—History—Colonial
period, ca. 1600–1775—Juvenile literature. I. Harkins, William H. II. Title. III. Building
America (Hockessin, Del.)
F234.J3H29 2006
975.5'02—dc22
                                                                                2005036497

ISBN-10:1-58415-458-6   ISBN-13: 978-1-58415-458-7

ABOUT THE AUTHOR: Susan and Bill Harkins live in Kentucky, where they enjoy writing together for children. Susan has written many books for adults and children. Bill is a history buff. In addition to writing, Bill is a member of the Kentucky Civil Air Patrol, where he helps Kentuckians prepare for earthquakes and other natural disasters.

PHOTO CREDITS: Cover, pp. 1, 3, 6, 9, 12—Getty Images; p. 15—Superstock; p. 17—Getty Images; pp. 20, 25, 28—North Wind Picture Archives; pp. 31, 34, 39—Getty Images.

PUBLISHER'S NOTE: This story is based on the authors' extensive research, which they believe to be accurate. Documentation of such research is contained on page 43.
        The internet sites referenced herein were active as of the publication date. Due to the fleeting nature of some web sites, we cannot guarantee they will all be active when you are reading this book.

PLB4

Contents

Chapter 1

England Sails to the New World 7

*FYInfo: The Virginia Company of London 11

Chapter 2

Fort James! 13

FYInfo: More About John Smith 19

Chapter 3

Fort James and the Powhatans 21

FYInfo: Exposing Pocahontas 27

Chapter 4

President Smith Rescues Fort James 29

FYInfo: The Rest of John Smith's Story 33

Chapter 5

Things Get Worse, Then Better 35

FYInfo: Virginia's Tobacco—The Road
to Riches and Slavery 42

Chapter Notes 43

Chronology 43

Timeline in History 45

Further Reading 46

    For Young Adults 46

    Works Consulted 46

    On the Internet 46

Glossary 46

Index 48

*For Your Information

Jamestown's first settlers survived a perilous four-month journey across the Atlantic Ocean. They were stuffed on board three small ships—the largest was the size of a three-bedroom house. Most of the men ate and slept on deck, regardless of the weather.

Chapter

England Sails to the New World

On December 19, 1606, a group of Englishmen watched London disappear through a gray mist. They were sailing down the Thames River to the English Channel. From there, they'd cross the Atlantic Ocean on their way to Virginia in the New World. Some of them probably grieved for what they were leaving behind and might never see again. Perhaps they were frightened about crossing the ocean. What they couldn't have known was how ill prepared they were for what lay ahead. Within nine months, two-thirds of them would be dead.

One-armed Captain Christopher Newport led the expedition to establish an English colony in North America from the flagship the *Susan Constant*. Years of fighting the Spanish as a privateer made him the Virginia Company of London's first choice for the perilous journey. John Ratcliffe captained the *Discovery*, and Bartholomew Gosnold captained the *Godspeed*. Of the three, only Captain Newport would survive their adventure.

A storm forced the captains to anchor just off the coast of England. The passengers were wet, cold, and miserable. Many were seasick; before long, the stench was unbearable. For almost a month, the boat tossed in the turbulent water, rocked by the storm's howling winds.

Fighting broke out as the men lost heart. Captains Gosnold and Ratcliffe wanted to return home. John Smith, a soldier and self-made man, wanted to wait out the storm and continue the voyage. The majority of men sided with Smith. Ratcliffe never forgot their slight.

The expedition was 105 men strong (with 39 crewmen). The passengers weren't soldiers or conquerors. Most were after treasure or land. A few, like the kindly Reverend Robert Hunt, wanted to save the souls of the native inhabitants by teaching them Christianity. Only a few, like Smith, were on board for the adventure. They were Englishmen—rich and poor, young and old—all bound for a new life.

Conditions were crowded and harsh. The *Discovery* was the size of a subway car and carried twenty-one men plus supplies. The *Godspeed* had fifty-two feet of usable deck space from end to end. It was smaller than the average modern house, and it carried fifty-one men and their supplies.

The crewmen were lucky to share small cabins below deck. A few of the more important gentlemen also had small private areas below deck. The hull, filled with food, tools, and weapons, had no room for the other passengers, who slept on deck.

With no running water or modern sanitation, the odor was bad within just a few days. By the end of the voyage, the smell of vomit and human waste was unbearable. The only thing worse than the smell was the food. Both the crew and the passengers ate stale, weevil-infested biscuits and dried meats. They drank mostly ale because the fresh water they brought with them spoiled quickly.

Finally, after four months at sea, the weary passengers caught sight of their new home. By the light of a waxing moon, near 4:00 A.M. on April 26, 1607, the three small vessels, flanked by Cape Charles and Cape Henry, sailed into a calm Chesapeake Bay. No one had the energy to celebrate.

At dawn, thirty men rowed ashore and hiked to the top of a sand dune. They watched and listened as the rising sun woke the untamed

The European settlers found a wilderness full of natural resources. Wild game and timber were abundant. Still, they were disappointed because they found no gold or silver.

forests of Virginia that lay at their feet. Unspoiled woods heavy with the scent of honeysuckle and teeming with game stretched before them as far as they could see. Dogwoods, flowers, and wild fruits sprinkled the dark green foliage with color. The woods rang with the songs of wild and brightly feathered birds that flew in the forest's canopy. The number of wild turkeys and deer astounded them. Sometime during the day, they thought they spotted a monkey, which turned out to be a raccoon. They'd never seen a raccoon before.

Despite Virginia's natural abundance and beauty, the men were disappointed. The company had promised them gold and silver, but as noted by colonist George Percy (also spelled *Percie*), they found none:

"Wee could find nothing worth the speaking of but faire med-dowes and goodly tall Trees."[1]

That night, by torchlight, the discouraged scouts returned to their rowboats rocking on the inlet's gentle waves. On the other side of the dunes, unseen and unheard, some native people hid. The small group of Paspahegh Indians had trailed the white men all day.

Once the strange white men were safe aboard their large winged boats, the wind would carry them like birds, down the river and into the Paspahegh villages. With loud whoops and flying arrows, five men sprang from their hiding place and ran down the sand dunes to attack the shore party. On board the anchored ships, the rest of the colonists witnessed the attack and quickly shot a cannon. Its earsplitting boom startled the Paspahegh, who retreated into the dark woods.

Smith, incarcerated aboard the *Susan Constant*, accused of plotting a mutiny, watched the attack. The Paspahegh, accurate with their arrows, wounded a few of the colonists with their simple weapons. The English had failed to hit a single target with their modern muskets. The Paspahegh were larger and stronger than the English. Everyone said the native people were no match for the civilized English, but Smith feared they were wrong.

The colonists had no way of knowing that they had landed in one of the most heavily populated communities on the eastern seacoast. Approximately fourteen thousand people lived in the area between the Chesapeake Bay and the James River Falls at present-day Richmond, Virginia.

The settlers had no idea what they faced. Over the next several months, hostile natives, disease, and starvation would claim the lives of most of these men.

The Virginia Company of London

Queen Elizabeth I

During the sixteenth century, English forays to the New World were few. Elizabeth I inherited a bankrupt country. She spent most of her reign at war with Spain. Sir Walter Raleigh established a colony at Roanoke Island in North Carolina, but the mysterious disappearance of all its inhabitants still baffles historians.

James I, Elizabeth's successor, was more interested in the New World than Elizabeth had been. In 1606, he awarded a charter to a group of investors who created The Virginia Company of London. Selling shares, they collected enough money to finance a voyage to the New World. Their goal was to establish a small settlement that would make a profit for the company. They also hoped to find a water passage through North America to the Pacific Ocean, which would make the trip to Asia's expensive spices and silks much quicker and safer. The colonists weren't a conquering army in the name of the English king, James I. Merchants owned Jamestown.

The company provided passage, arms, clothing, and food for anyone willing to work in Virginia. In truth, the agreement was a form of indentured servitude, but land and treasure were strong motivators. Unfortunately, scandal was often the company's main business. It started a lottery in 1612 and collected over 29,000 pounds sterling (British monetary units), but the lottery's manager took it for himself. From 1615 to 1617, they collected money to build a school for Virginia's native peoples, but the company used the funds to pay for supplies instead.

Many fell for the company's get-rich schemes of finding gold and silver. Others wanted freedom—there were few opportunities to better one's life in England. Some were adventurers, driven by the love of new experiences. Few met the challenge.

After a few days of exploring, the Jamestown settlers chose an island for their fort. They unloaded their supplies and began building Fort James.

Chapter

Fort James!

Despite the frightful end to the shore party's day, emotions were high on board the *Susan Constant*. It was time to open the sealed box that contained instructions for the colonists. Those contents named seven men to the colony's first governing council. Edward-Maria Wingfield, Christopher Newport, Bartholomew Gosnold, John Ratcliffe, George Kendall, and John Martin were no surprise. The seventh member, John Smith, was a prisoner for supposedly plotting mutiny. The other members rejected Smith's appointment.

The colony's main objective was to make money for the company's investors. In addition, they were to seek a water passage to the Pacific Ocean. For the actual settlement, they were advised to choose a spot far from the ocean—as far as one hundred miles inland from the Chesapeake Bay—to lessen the chance of a surprise attack by the Spanish. The men were disappointed to learn that they couldn't return to England without the council's permission. Nor could they send home unfavorable news of the colony.

After reading their instructions, Captain Newport's men built a small boat known as a shallop. They would use it to explore the inland waterways. They didn't know it at the time, but the area's waterways were the perfect highway system. A network of streams, flowing in all directions, penetrated the deep forests for almost one hundred miles.

They spent several days exploring the James River (which they named after James I). Along the way, they met many friendly native people. Eventually, they found a small peninsula surrounded by deep water. A narrow land bridge, which the river covered at high tide, was its only connection to the mainland. They'd have no trouble defending the site from the Spanish or the native peoples (or so they thought). There seemed to be no inhabitants there to appease or offend, and wild game was plentiful. On May 13, 1607, the colonists began moving their provisions to the island. They called their settlement Fort James.

The council's next action was to elect Edward-Maria Wingfield to a one-year term as president. As an educated gentleman, he seemed the most likely candidate. Unfortunately, forging a colony in the Virginia wilderness required a leader with common sense. They needed a leader who knew the value of manual labor, and that certainly wasn't Wingfield. He started making mistakes right away.

Trying to present a passive presence to the people living near them, Wingfield decided not to build a wall around the fort. He even refused to unpack their weapons. The company had warned the colonists not to harm or offend these people in their instructions: "In all your passages you must have great care not to offend the naturals."[1]

Most everyone, including Smith, disagreed with Wingfield.

On May 21, Captain Newport took twenty-three men and began his search for a river route to the Pacific Ocean. Only five of the men, one of which was John Smith, were colonists. The rest were seamen from Newport's crews. (John Smith was still under arrest, but the group needed every man to work. He wasn't locked aboard the ship any longer.)

The colony's fifty-four gentlemen were unprepared for the realities of the wilderness. When choosing recruits, the London Company had been less than practical. They sent men of noble birth and social position—gentlemen—to settle the Virginia wilderness. Smith wasn't impressed with them. He wrote they were "ten times more fit to spoil a commonwealth than either to begin one or help to maintain one."[2]

The men encountered many villages along the river. The people there lived in houses made of reeds, covered with tree bark and thatch roofs. A grass mat covered each house's single entry. More mats hung from the roofs outside, providing shade and protection similar to a porch. Small groups of these houses dotted each village, usually under trees for protection.

A few days into their mapless journey, the explorers shared a meal with a friendly Algonquin tribe. For the first time, the settlers heard of Powhatan, the great chief who would be both their salvation and their nemesis over the next decade.

Powhatan was a demanding chief who ruled from a village on the York River, just north of the James River. His empire covered what is now eastern Virginia. His men were strong hunters and warriors—and deadly accurate at both. Boys trained with the bow and

Powhatan Indians lived along the many rivers that flow inland from the Chesapeake Bay. They made their houses out of reeds and bark. The Jamestown settlers visited many of these villages and traded goods with the local tribes.

arrow starting at age six. Only after they practiced would their mothers feed them breakfast.

The men and children in these villages were mostly naked, except for a single patch of leather to protect the groin. The men decorated their bodies with animal bones and feathers. Some painted themselves—no two were ever alike. Some hung bird legs from their ears. They wore their straight black hair long on the left side, tied with feathers. In contrast, they shaved the right side close to the scalp. Later, the colonists learned that the men shaved the right side of their heads to keep from tangling their hair in their hunting bows.

The English colonists had no experience with the Powhatans. The friendly visits gave the colonists a false sense of security. Understandably, Captain Newport was shocked when he returned to Fort James on May 27, 1607, and learned that warriors had attacked the colony the day before. Several men were wounded; at least one man died. (Sources disagree on the number of dead.) Cannonfire from the anchored ships scared the warriors, who retreated.

Smith criticized the council for leaving the colonists in such danger. For this, he won the affection and respect of most of the colonists, who forced the council to allow Smith to take his seat. The group immediately went to work surrounding the fort with walls of thick, upright logs. They shaved the tip of each upright log into a sharp point. Fortifications included a cannon in each corner.

They couldn't work fast enough, though. Over the next few days, warriors continued to attack the fort, killing at least two more colonists. By June 15, the colonists finished their triangular fortress.

Captain Newport failed to find a route to the west, but the hull of his ship was filled with clapboard when he sailed for England that June. He also carried letters that described fertile land, bountiful rivers, and friendly native peoples waiting to be "civilized." Of course, the men exaggerated; they needed the company's support, so they couldn't be entirely truthful. They never forgot that the company might abandon the venture, and them, at any time.

President Wingfield's priorities were questionable from the beginning. The men cut clapboard for the company instead of build-

The settlers built Fort James on the banks of a small island. It was triangular with a wall of wooden logs set upright. The channel was deep and the ships could dock right outside the gate.

ing shelters for themselves. With the surrounding woods full of food, they went hungry. The Paspahegh, who claimed the island as theirs, were hostile to the settlers. Wingfield made little effort to improve relations with them. Soon, daily rations were down to a half pint of boiled barley and a half pint of wheat, both spoiled by worms. John Smith wrote: "At this time our diet was for the most part water and bran, and three ounces of little better stuffe in bread for five men a meale, and thus we lived neere three months: our lodgings under boughs of trees, the savages being our enemies, whom we neither knew nor understood; occasion I thinke sufficient to make men sicke and die."[3]

Although starving, they did have religion. The Reverend Hunt called them to prayer twice a day and preached two sermons every Sunday.

All too soon, nature replaced spring's mild breezes with summer's sweltering heat. Used to England's mild summers, the men had only their English woolen clothes. They discovered that their easily defensible and accessible island was actually a mosquito-filled swamp.

The river shimmered in the sun, but at low tide, it was full of living slime. With the heat and summer tides, the river had turned brackish. The men begin to dehydrate.

Poor nutrition and disease—the reward for their leaders' inexperience—began claiming victims. The diseased men fell silent as they roasted in the intense heat. At one point, only five men were well enough to stand guard, nurse the sick, and bury the dead.

Some were lethargic from lack of good food and water. Many were bloated from salt poisoning (from drinking the river water). Others suffered from chills and high fevers. Most likely, these colonists suffered from malaria and dysentery, brought by the summer's mosquitos and aggravated by bad food and foul water. George Percy wrote of this time: "The sixth of August there died John Asbie of the bloody flux. . . . The ninth died George Flower of the swelling. The tenth died William Bruster, Gentleman, of a wound given by the savages. . . . The 14th, Jerome Alicock . . . died of a wound."[4]

That August, nineteen men died of disease or from wounds inflicted by the natives (probably Paspahegh). Morale was low, and the men blamed their leaders.

President Wingfield avoided both illness and starvation—he was the only colonist to not fall sick during that first summer. Winfield's good health made him the target of gossip and suspicion. On September 10, the council relieved Wingfield and sent him to live on the *Discovery*. They elected John Ratcliffe their new president.

The whole affair shook up the council. They realized that their original goals had been shortsighted and naive. They must learn how to get along with the people who had lived there before them. More importantly, they must learn quickly or die.

More About John Smith

John Smith was born into a respectable English family of farmers in 1580. He attended grammar school but dreamed of adventure. Struck with wanderlust, he tried to run away from home at thirteen. At fifteen, he apprenticed to a merchant. When his father died, Smith left his apprenticeship and became a solider in the Netherlands' war of independence from Spain.

After the war, he returned to England and studied munitions. A grown man now, he was short, stocky, and tough. He wore a full beard and mustache.

John Smith

In 1601, he fought against the Muslim Turks in Hungary, where he soon made captain. The Turks took him prisoner in 1602 and auctioned him for a slave. His new master shaved his head and clapped a ring of iron around his neck. Instead of a respected captain, he was just one of many slaves. Escape looked impossible.

One day the master made the mistake of riding too close to Smith. Smith pulled him from his horse and beat him to death. He rode off in the master's clothes on the master's horse. On his journey home, a Polish prince heard of Smith's escape and granted him a coat of arms, which bears three Turks' heads and the motto "To conquer—to overcome—is to live."[5]

By the time he joined the Jamestown expedition, he was confident and daring. He was just the type of person the expedition needed. His military experience and his years spent among foreigners—both as friend and foe—shaped a man few English gentlemen could match.

Unfortunately for Smith, he spent most of the trip locked up for supposedly plotting a mutiny. There was no evidence that he wanted to start an uprising. When Smith refused to treat the socially superior gentlemen as betters, Wingfield convinced Captain Newport to clap Smith in chains and confine him below deck.

Despite the rough start, Smith later proved worthy to be the colony's leader. In fact, he proved to be the only competent leader during those early years when survival was the toughest challenge.

Most of what we know of Smith comes from his own writings, so there's always the possibility that he embellished his life somewhat. However, his contemporaries accepted his colonial stories as truthful renditions of their shared experiences. In addition, the coat of arms is real, which helps make his story credible.

FYI

★★★ For Your Information

Powhatan's people were generous with the food they grew in their village. Many times during the first few years of the colony, the Powhatans were all that stood between the settlers and starvation. The Europeans traded goods such as kettles and beads for food.

Chapter

③

Fort James and the Powhatans

President Ratcliffe took over the group of demoralized and starving men. Several miles off, the great chief Powhatan considered the white men. He didn't want to attack the weakened fort, lest they take revenge. He also thought about his native enemies, who for the time being were more concerned with the English than with him. Eventually, he might form an alliance with the English against them. Most likely, Powhatan decided to use the English to his advantage. He sent them food instead of letting them starve to death.

When Captain Newport didn't return from England in November as expected, Smith sailed up the Chickahominy River seeking food and a western water route. About fifty miles into the trip, the river became too shallow for the shallop. He and his crew stopped at a small village, where Smith found two native people willing to guide him and two of his men upriver in a canoe.

The rest of Smith's men remained on the shallop, anchored near the village. Despite Smith's strict orders not to leave the boat, the men disobeyed when a small group of Powhatan women came down to greet them. Once the Englishmen were on shore, warriors attacked them. After a short skirmish, all but one of the settlers made it back to the shallop.

From the shallop, the Englishmen watched the villagers strip George Cassen of his clothes and tie him to a pair of wooden stakes. Using mussel shells, they cut each of his fingers, joint by joint, and then tossed each piece into the fire. On board the shallop, the men could hear Cassen's agonizing screams as the villagers skinned him alive. Then, they watched in horror as the villagers sliced open his belly and removed his bowels, which they threw into the fire. Finally, they burned the nearly dead Cassen alive.

Meanwhile, Smith was hunting birds with one of the guides, having no knowledge of what was going on at the village. Just a few minutes into his hunt, he heard a loud war whoop from the direction of the shore where he'd left his two companions and the other guide. Smith's guide urged him to run, but an arrow struck Smith's thigh.

Using his guide as a shield, Smith tried to make his way back to the river. He stepped backward into a marsh and found himself stuck in a bog. Surrounded by warriors, Smith surrendered his pistol. Soon, he was standing in front of Opechancanough, third in the line of succession to the great chief Powhatan.

Thinking quickly, Smith showed his captors his compass. Watching the needle always point in the same direction, they suspected Smith was a man of magic and sent him to the great chief, Powhatan. Most likely, Opechancanough didn't want the responsibility of deciding such a powerful man's fate.

On December 30, Smith became the first white man to meet the great Powhatan chief. He entered the chief's lodge and waited for his eyes to adjust in the darkness. In front of the fire, he saw an old man with gray hair sitting on a stack of straw mats. The chief was tall and physically fit. Smith guessed him to be between sixty and seventy years old. (Powhatan wasn't the chief's given name; he was called Powhatan as the chief of that tribe.)

Young girls sat beside the chief. Men stood on either side of the fire, and more young girls stood behind the men. Someone shoved Smith forward, and the group of men and girls shouted in unison.

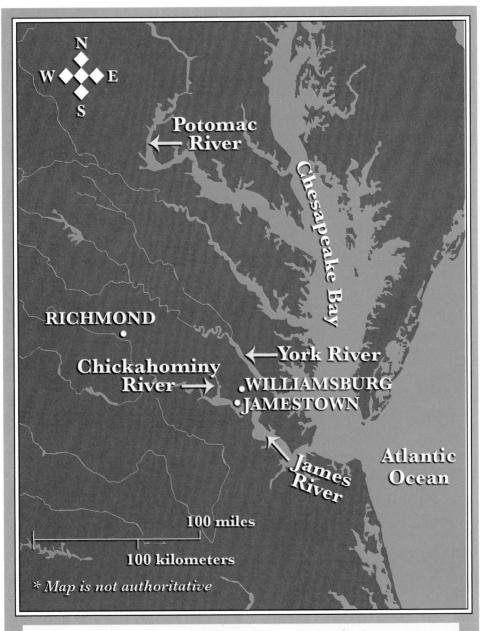

The Jamestown settlers sailed up the James River to find the perfect spot for their fort. Powhatan's village was north of Jamestown, on the York River. Captain Newport and John Smith both explored the James and York Rivers looking for the Northwest Passage. Williamsburg (Middle Plantation) and Richmond would be settled much later.

Powhatan seemed to consider his options. Smith didn't know it, but the Powhatans had a custom of keeping the chiefs of enemy tribes as servants. Powhatan believed Smith to be a chief. Perhaps he also considered the possibility of an alliance and getting his hands on English weapons.

On the other hand, perhaps these English were the people his priests had referred to years before. A priest had once warned him that people from the bay area would invade Powhatan's lands and destroy his people. After hearing this, Powhatan sent his fiercest men to destroy a tribe living in the bay area. It is possible that Powhatan wondered if these white settlers were the ones from the warning instead.

Powhatan seemed to make his choice. Two large men shoved Smith to his knees and forced his head down on two flat stones. Other men lifted large wooden clubs into the air, but before they could smash Smith's skull, a small girl rushed forward. She begged Powhatan to spare Smith's life. Powhatan agreed. That young girl was Powhatan's favorite daughter, Matoaka, whom he called Pocahontas, or "naughty one."

Two days later, Powhatan freed Smith with instructions to send back two cannons and a grindstone from the fort. Smith left Powhatan's village knowing he wouldn't fulfill the chief's request. Not only would the villagers use those weapons against other tribes, they might use the weapons against the colonists.

This cannon incident was the beginning of an ongoing game of wits between the two adversaries. Powhatan believed he would get the white man's weapons. For his part, Smith appeared agreeable to trading cannons for his life. In the end, the Powhatans were unable to carry the cannons back to their village. They were too heavy, and the journey through the forest was too long. That January, 1608, the native men took many gifts from the fort back to Powhatan, but they didn't return with the cannons that Powhatan coveted.

Smith faced another challenge at the fort. Keeping to its pattern of arrogance and stupidity, the council accused Smith of deliberately leading the men into a trap and to their deaths. They sentenced him to death and planned to hang him the next day. Ratcliffe was behind the accusation and hoped to get rid of Smith.

When John Smith was forced to lay his head on a stone for execution, Powhatan's daughter, Pocahontas, begged for his life. She was just 10 or 11, but she was the great chief's favorite child, so he agreed. John Smith and Pocahontas became good friends over the next few years.

Miraculously, Captain Newport arrived from England that same January evening with fresh supplies. He immediately freed Smith, who walked away from certain death for the second time in just a few days.

Captain Newport was discouraged to find only thirty-eight men still alive at the fort. As so often happened at the fort, things were about to get worse. A fire destroyed most of their crude houses and their provisions—including all the new supplies Captain Newport had brought.

This was especially troublesome since the captain had also brought 120 new settlers. Now, 158 men had almost no food.

Once again, the colonists turned to the Powhatans for help. Ratcliffe was jealous of Smith's relations with the native people. In an attempt to undermine him, he willingly offered too much too early in the negotiations. Instead of undermining Smith, he introduced inflation, and the colony would suffer for it over the coming months. Not only would the colonists pay unreasonably high prices for grain, the Powhatans came to view them as weak for paying too much.

Pocahontas began to visit Smith at the fort regularly. She taught the young boys at the fort how to cartwheel. Smith taught Pocahontas English; she taught him her native tongue. Pocahontas often brought food, and Smith always had a small gift of beads or bells for her. He owed the young girl his life. Beyond that, he also admired her spirit, intelligence, and wit. Smith's friendship with Pocahontas helped improve relations with Powhatan.

During this time, Captain Newport's sailors dug for gold and ate what little food the colony managed to trade for. In April, Captain Newport left for England with a hull full of gold and cedar. That summer (1608), President Ratcliffe ordered the settlers to pan for gold instead of cutting timber. To everyone's disappointment, the ore turned out to be pyrite, or fool's gold.

Smith explored and mapped the Chesapeake Bay. When he returned in late July, he found the men sick with swamp fever. President Ratcliffe ate while the men built a palace for him.

Smith took over immediately.

Exposing Pocahontas

Storytellers tend to romanticize the relationship between John Smith and Pocahontas. The truth is that she was a child of ten or eleven when they first met. She was still roaming the forest mostly naked, as the Powhatan children did. She certainly wasn't old enough to be a love interest for twenty-seven-year-old Smith.

Pocahontas

We know from Smith's writings that Pocahontas asked her father to spare Smith's life and the old chief agreed. Smith claimed the child saved him out of compassion.

Over the years, some historians have tried to discredit the story, but the evidence suggests that the incident actually occurred. Perhaps, most importantly, John Smith's contemporaries accepted the story and recommended his writings as truthful renditions of their shared experiences in Virginia.

Some historians believe that Smith mistook an adoption ceremony for his execution. This explanation seems unlikely. Powhatan demanded English goods in exchange for Smith's freedom. It's possible that tradition required an adopted member of the tribe to give gifts, but Smith's writings don't make that connection. Considering that Smith and Pocahontas continued to behave courteously, and were even friendly, toward one another for the next few years, it seems unlikely that such a misunderstanding would have persisted. In addition, Pocahontas often referred to Smith as "father." If Powhatan had adopted Smith, she would've called him brother.

Another possibility is that Powhatan prearranged the entire scene with his daughter. Powhatan didn't want the settlers dead. He wanted their weapons. Putting John Smith in the position to buy his freedom might have been a ruse to gain guns and swords. However, if Pocahontas or Powhatan ever admitted as much, that admission never made it into Smith's memoirs.

From Smith's own writings, we know that he cared for Pocahontas. He admired her lively spirit and gave her the nickname Nonpareil, which is French for "having no equal." His writings also suggest that she returned his friendship, which has withstood history's scrutiny.

FYI

For Your Information

Women didn't make the trip to Jamestown at first. Starting in the fall of 1608, single women came to be colonists' wives. All worked and occasionally starved alongside their new husbands.

Chapter

4

President Smith Rescues Fort James

Under Smith's leadership, conditions inside the fort began to improve. The men harvested their crops and built new houses. However, they continued to die from disease, and hostile natives living nearby continued to harass them.

Captain Newport arrived in September with new colonists and supplies, including the colony's first two women. He also returned with a problem. Showing just how little the English understood native culture, the company wanted Captain Newport to crown Powhatan an English prince. The goal was to flatter the chief while making him a subject of King James.

Powhatan wasn't keen on the idea, but Captain Newport brought many presents to the coronation: a bed, a washbasin and pitcher, a cloak, and a pair of shoes. The ceremony had unintended consequences. Powhatan stopped trading, which came at a bad time for the colonists. The company had tired of supporting the colonists and demanded that they feed themselves by hunting, fishing, and trading. Captain Newport had brought no food on this return trip. Amazingly, there weren't enough skilled fishermen and hunters among the colonists to feed them all.

This turn of events helped Powhatan. He knew the English were starving. If they got hungry enough, they might agree to trade weapons for food. Powhatan offered to fill the *Discovery* with food. All he wanted in return was an English house, a grindstone, a rooster and hen, copper, beads, guns, and swords. Smith knew they could never give the Powhatans guns and swords, and the negotiating began.

Smith sent men to start on Powhatan's house. Then he set sail on the *Discovery*. On the way to the village, a lesser chief of a village en route warned Smith that Powhatan planned to kill him.

When Smith arrived at Powhatan's village, the chief demanded that Smith's men disarm, but Smith refused. When Smith tried to leave, Powhatan's braves stopped him at the door. Smith's men fired warning shots into the air, alerting the men on the ship, who ran quickly to the village.

Smith's armed men faced Powhatan's braves—each waiting for the other to move. In the end, Powhatan defused the situation by telling Smith that the braves were there only to protect his corn. They didn't want to kill Smith and his men. Smith didn't believe Powhatan, but he didn't want to fight either.

Finally, Powhatan and Smith's men loaded the *Discovery* with grain, but it was too late in the evening to leave. Smith's party would have to wait out the night in a shelter on shore.

Pocahontas soon appeared at the shelter, having traveled through the dark woods alone. She warned Smith that warriors would soon arrive with food. While Smith and his men ate, the warriors would kill them. If that failed, Powhatan would send a larger group to kill them while they slept. Smith had nothing to give Pocahontas, so he offered her beads and other trinkets as a thank-you. Through tears, Pocahontas refused the beads. If caught with them, her father would know what she'd done. She then disappeared into the darkness. Smith would not see the child again for many years, and by then she would be a grown woman with a young child of her own.

History doesn't explain Pocahontas' actions. She committed treason against her father to save Smith. If caught, Powhatan might

If not for the Powhatan Indians, the Jamestown settlers would have starved to death. Powhatan, the great chief, wanted to trade food for English weapons. He never got them from the Jamestown settlers.

have executed her. We know from Smith's writings that the two were good friends, but she took a huge risk that night to save Smith and his men. However, historians widely accept the story as true, even though they don't understand Powhatan's or Pocahontas' motives. It is clear that we don't know the whole story.

When a group of Powhatan men appeared with food, Smith insisted that they taste it to make sure it wasn't poisoned. Then he sent the food bearers back with a message for Powhatan—Smith and his men were waiting for his warriors. A second attack never came.

The next day, Smith returned to the fort with food and a new rule: Settlers must work to eat. That winter, under Smith's leadership, the men built several new houses and dug a well inside the fort.

About this time the company executives in London changed a few of their policies. They decided to do away with the council and put a single man in charge. They selected Lord De La Warr (pronounced DEH leh wayr) as Virginia's first governor.

They continued to collect money from investors, but instead of paying dividends, they promised land—a hundred acres per share. The company sent nine ships and five hundred new settlers to Virginia that summer.

In August 1609, several English ships arrived with three hundred settlers and provisions. The senior men among the new arrivals demanded that Smith step down. Smith demanded to see the new charter relieving him of duty. Fortunately for Smith, those orders were on board the *Sea Venture* with the new lieutenant governor, Sir Thomas Gates, and that ship was missing. (Lord De La Warr sent Gates, his lieutenant governor, over first.)

Smith's days at the colony were limited, but not because the new leadership was able to unseat him. His powder bag, hanging from his belt, caught fire and burned him. The wound was severe and he was in agony. Since there was no doctor, he decided to return to England for treatment.

Unfortunately for Smith, the new council, intent on condemning him, retained his ship for almost a month while they tried to coerce statements that would convict him on some misdeed. They were unsuccessful, but for that month, the fort was idle. Condemning Smith was more important to the new leaders than the fort or its inhabitants. Knowing that Smith was lying aboard the ship in agony seemed of no consequence whatsoever.

In October 1609, Smith left behind almost five hundred colonists. George Percy would be in charge until Gates arrived. The colonists told the Powhatans that Smith was dead. Pocahontas, hearing the news, didn't return to the fort for several years. Smith never returned to Fort James. For the remaining settlers, the worst was yet to come.

The Rest of John Smith's Story

John Smith left the Virginia colony when he was twenty-nine after spending only two years there. While there he established good relations with the Powhatans. He learned their language and their customs. He also mapped a large part of the Chesapeake Bay area now known as Tidewater. The company never granted him permission to return to the colony.

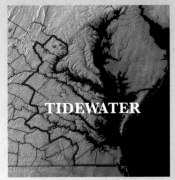

A map of the Tidewater area

While in Virginia, Smith kept meticulous notes. Back in England, he collected his notes into a book, which included sketches of his maps. In 1612, he published his collection, titled *A Map of Virginia: With a Description of the Countrey, the Commodities, People, Government and Religion.*

Twice, Smith made it back to North America. On March 3, 1614, he commanded two ships sailing for New England. The expedition was to look for gold and copper and to hunt whales. Smith took the opportunity to map the coast of Maine.

In 1615 he returned with the intentions of colonizing New England, but he never made it. French privateers menaced his ships until Smith met with the French captain. While he was negotiating with the privateers, his own men mutinied and abandoned him to the French.

The French tried to force Smith to sign a paper acquitting them of any crime. As privateers, they had permission from the French crown to attack Spanish and Portuguese ships, but not English ones. Smith refused and escaped in a small rowboat during a storm. Hunters found him the next morning. Smith was more fortunate than his French captors, who wrecked on a reef that same night. While on board the French vessel, Smith had started a book titled *A Description of New England,* which he published the next summer (1616), about the same time Pocahontas and John Rolfe landed in England.

Smith's vision for America was enlightened for the times. He saw a country of freedom where a man could decide his destiny and pursue his interests. In his *Generall Historie,* Smith condemned the Virginia Company of London's practice of keeping a common food store and maintaining authoritarian rule. He encouraged private ownership of land.

John Smith died in England on June 21, 1631, at fifty-one years old. He left no survivors and no fortune other than his writings.

The King of England tried to crown Powhatan as a prince. Captain Newport crowned the chief, even though the old man resisted. The king offered friendship, but really wanted to control the chief.

Chapter

5

Things Get Worse, Then Better

George Percy was a nobleman and intelligent, but unprepared for the task put before him. One of his first mistakes was to send Ratcliffe to trade with Powhatan.

Ratcliffe didn't understand the Powhatans as Smith had, and his ignorance proved fatal. Upon meeting the great chief Powhatan, Ratcliffe failed to follow protocol. He should have demanded that Powhatan trade hostages. (It was common for both sides to have a few captives.) His failure to make this crucial step sealed his fate. Powhatan didn't tolerate weak men like Ratcliffe.

There are two tales of Ratcliffe's tragic end. In one, the Powhatans cheated the settlers while trading. When Ratcliffe complained, the Powhatans killed all the traders. A second story claims Ratcliffe allowed his men to wander off in small groups, and the Powhatans picked them off a few at a time.

We do know what happened to Ratcliffe. From an anchored ship, his men watched the Powhatans tie Ratcliffe to a stake in front of a large fire. Women skinned him alive and threw his flesh into the fire. Then they burned him alive.

After killing Ratcliffe, the Powhatans attacked the ship. Fifty men left Jamestown, hoping to trade food; sixteen men returned empty-handed.

Powhatan had respected Smith. Their relationship kept the two communities in an uneasy peace. With Smith gone, Powhatan's warriors intimidated the settlers with small raids to keep them inside their settlement. They slaughtered their wild hogs. They released their boats from their moors so that the Englishmen couldn't escape.

The colony's storehouses were empty. The remaining colonists faced that winter with almost no food. They ate their horses, their cats, and even their dogs. Then, they ate rats and mice. Some ate their shoe leather and made porridge from laundry starch. They even resorted to cannibalism when they dug up and ate the corpse of a Powhatan they had killed and buried just a few days before.

Only a few resorted to such desperate measures, probably driven insane by their hunger. A few colonists dug their own graves and laid down in them to die. The colonists came to call the winter of 1609 to 1610 the Starving Time.

It's true that many starved to death, but the real killers were poor leadership, a lack of ambition to save themselves, and fear. That spring President Percy found some men who'd gone downriver to the oyster beds, living well off crabs and wild hogs.

It's hard to know who got the biggest surprise in May 1610 when survivors of the missing *Sea Venture* sailed up the James River. A hurricane had stranded the ship in Bermuda, where the survivors found plenty of food and fresh water. The castaways, including Thomas Gates, the lieutenant governor De La Warr had sent over first, built new ships and sailed to Virginia. In Fort James, the new arrivals found utter misery and only sixty emaciated colonists. Unfortunately for everyone, the voyagers had packed only enough food to make the voyage.

Gates decided to abandon the colony. On June 7, 1610, the retreating fleet met a small boat with one passenger, who presented a letter to acting governor Gates. The letter was from Lord De La Warr.

He was at the Chesapeake Bay encampment (the one that had survived so well during the Starving Time). The letter ordered the frustrated group back to Fort James. Lord De La Warr's ships held enough food to feed everyone for a year.

Governor De La Warr found the fort vile and unwholesome. Within days he was ill. Ironically, Governor for Life De La Warr lasted just nine months in the colony. He returned to England in March of 1611.

Governor Thomas Dale arrived with three hundred new colonists and took De La Warr's post. He was a harsh administrator. Execution was the punishment for even small transgressions. Dale had deserters hung, burned at the stake, or shot. Thieves were tied to trees and left to starve.

Although harsh to the colonists, Dale repaired relations with the Powhatans and soon the colonists were trading with friendly groups on the Potomac River. During one of these trading trips, Samuel Argall conspired with Japazeus, chief of the Patawomeck, to kidnap Pocahontas and hold her for ransom. Japazeus and his wife tricked Pocahontas into boarding Argall's ship. Once she was on board, Argall sailed away. For his part, Japazeus got a copper kettle—a great prize to the natives. Powhatan paid the ransom, but Pocahontas never returned to her native home.

During captivity, Pocahontas lived with a minister and his wife. She eventually converted to Christianity, taking Rebecca as her new name. No longer a captive, but living at Jamestown of her own free will, she married John Rolfe, an English planter and one of the first to experiment with tobacco.

By this time, the colony was a true settlement and no longer just a small triangular fort. When Governor Dale turned Jamestown over to George Yeardley in 1616, there were four hundred settlers living in four settlements: Jamestown, Henrico, Kecoughtan, and Dale's Gift.

That same year, seeking to exploit Pocahontas' conversion to Christianity, the company requested the Rolfes visit England. When

Smith learned of her visit, he wrote a letter of introduction to Queen Anne, in which he credited the young girl for saving his life twice:

> At the minute of my execution, she hazarded the beating out of her owne braines to save mine; and not onely that, but so prevailed with her father that I was safely conducted to James towne.[1]

The queen saw to it that her courtiers treated the native "princess" well during her visit. The title of *princess* was strictly an English convention; there was no such designation in the Powhatan hierarchy. In England, Pocahontas met John Smith one last time.

Pocahontas never returned to Virginia. She died in England on March 21, 1617—she was just twenty-one. Historians disagree on the cause of her death. Some think it was smallpox, others believe she died of tuberculosis or pneumonia. Her father, the great chief Powhatan, died a year later, in the spring of 1618.

In 1618, the company started a new program, known as the headright system, which awarded fifty acres to every person who paid his own passage. Once in Jamestown, the people had to find the land themselves and stake a claim, but that was better than any Englishman could hope for in England.

Fraud became an integral part of the headright program. Settlers often applied more than once. The program extended to servants as well, so settlers brought as many servants with them as they could. Even convicts got into the land business using this program. Despite the number of settlers entering the program, few actually succeeded. Many died in poverty or returned to England. Many found themselves tricked into indentured servitude instead of being new landowners.

Through the program, Jamestown and the surrounding settlements grew enough to become unruly. The company decided it was time for the settlers to govern themselves, and the change from martial law to representatives took place on July 30, 1619. Governor Yeardley presided over the first legislative assembly ever convened in North America. They called themselves the House of Burgesses. The group comprised the governor, six counselors, and two burgesses from each

Jamestown's settlers held the first legislative assembly in the New World. These representatives called their assembly the House of Burgesses. They met in the town's small church.

settlement. During this first meeting, which took place in the Jamestown church, the representatives passed laws against idleness, gaming, and drunkenness.

By 1621, tobacco plantations lined 140 miles of the James River, and 1,200 settlers called Virginia home. Women and children—families—were stabilizing the area. Sir Francis Wyatt replaced Yeardley as governor in 1621, and his job seemed an easy one. As he described it, he "found the country in very great amity and confidence with the natives."[2]

As the settlers became more secure, the Powhatans began to face reality. The white settlers were invaders. On March 22, 1622, Powhatan warriors killed 347 men, women, and children. Among the dead was John Rolfe, Pocahontas' widower. That year, 600 settlers died, but the company sent 800 replacements.

39

The attack changed the English attitude toward the Chesapeake Bay–area natives forever. Over the next two years, the English sent many raiding parties into native towns. The assault was broad; the settlers attacked many tribes, not just the Powhatans. The English burned the native villages and stole their food.

James I, disillusioned by the 1622 massacre, revoked the company's charter on May 24, 1624. That action made Virginia a royal colony. James I felt the company had overstepped its bounds by establishing the House of Burgesses. He feared sedition was growing in the colony. Understandably, the colonists fought the decision, but their protests were useless.

Despite the political upheaval, the next decade was prosperous for Virginians. By 1627, there were 1,500 settlers and 50 plantations along the James River. There were almost no native people.

Colonists continued to move inland, settling along the many tributaries that feed the Chesapeake Bay. Plantation houses, wharves, tobacco fields, and curing barns replaced the untamed forest. Even the poorest families had a small patch of land and some livestock. Indentured servants could eventually own land. In fact, in 1629, seven of the burgesses were ex-servants. Virginia was a land of possibilities—at least for the white settlers.

The Great Rebellion of 1640 pitted Oliver Cromwell against King Charles. Progressive leaders abolished trade restrictions and taxes. The House of Burgesses began electing its councilors and governor. The new freedoms didn't last long. Along with the Stuart line of kings, taxes and royally appointed governors returned.

The changes fueled loyalist Sir William Berkeley, a Stuart-appointed governor. He refused to allow any elections to the House of Burgesses.

Nathaniel Bacon, a young lawyer, led a rebellion against the corrupt governor in 1676. At first, he asked only to lead an expedition against warring natives who had attacked many plantations, including his own. Berkeley resisted at first, but in the end came to terms with Bacon. In a daring nighttime face-off, Bacon squeezed a few other concessions from the governor:

*Council members had to pay taxes like everyone else.

*Freemen could vote, even if they owned no land.

*Citizens would elect members of the county court.

*Berkeley had to reduce the number of people holding office.

Berkeley double-crossed Bacon and sent the militia after him, but Bacon's rebels were successful in temporarily ridding the colony of Berkeley's corrupt influence. When Bacon died in October, soon after he took Berkeley's place, a vengeful Berkeley executed every rebel he could find.

Virginians didn't gain much from the rebellion, as England recalled Berkeley and repealed Bacon's laws. However, it was clear that Virginians were a different breed of Englishmen. They were willing to die for their rights.

The restrictive rule of the Stuart kings ended in 1688 when the Glorious Revolution sent James II into exile. The new King William sent Francis Nicholson to Virginia; he was a sympathetic lieutenant governor.

During these later years, a small settlement called Middle Plantation began to come into its own. The small village had exploded with commerce after The College of William and Mary opened there. In 1699, the settlement caught the attention of the General Assembly. They liked it so much that they moved the capital from Jamestown to Middle Plantation. They changed the town's name to Williamsburg in honor of the new king. Williamsburg became the colony's main city, and Jamestown never recovered.

As new settlers arrived and the English claimed more and more land, Jamestown disappeared completely. In the twentieth century, archaeologists began excavating a site believed to be the original fort on the James River. Perhaps as they recover artifacts they see a ghost of a Powhatan child cartwheeling through the encampment. Jamestown's houses may be gone, but the spirit of those first colonists and natives lives on in our history and our hearts.

Virginia's Tobacco—The Road to Riches and Slavery

Virginia struggled financially until the settlers started experimenting with tobacco. Some might go so far as to suggest that tobacco saved Virginia.

John Rolfe, Pocahontas' husband, was one of the first planters to experiment with tobacco. The native species was harsh, so he created hybrids using tobacco seeds he brought with him from Bermuda. (He had been on the shipwrecked *Sea Venture*.) In England,

Tobacco Leaves

the hybrid tobacco went for three shillings a pound, and Virginia quickly became a one-crop colony. In 1616, Virginians exported 2,500 pounds of tobacco. By 1628, they were exporting over one million pounds a year.

Tobacco was a troublesome crop despite the fact that it made many Virginians rich. It depleted the soil, and it was labor-intensive. Raising tobacco took skill and hard work. At first, the planters used indentured servants, but servants had a way of fulfilling their contracts and leaving. Consequently, planters were constantly replacing and retraining servants.

The first slaves sailed into Jamestown in 1619 on the Dutch ship the *White Lion.* For a while, black slaves and white servants worked the plantations together. It was just a matter of time, though, before the planters saw the economic advantages of slavery. Planters preferred slaves because they were cheaper to keep and they reproduced, constantly replenishing the workforce. Unlike the indentured servants who worked toward freedom, a slave was a slave for life.

We do know that some of the black Africans, who arrived before the first slaves, eventually bought or earned their freedom. In fact, historians believe that the first blacks in America were actually indentured servants and not slaves.

Chapter Notes

Chapter 1
England Sails to the New World

1. Price, David A., *Love and Hate in Jamestown* (New York: Alfred A. Knopf, 2003), p. 28.

Chapter 2
Fort James!

1. Morgan, Ted, *Wilderness at Dawn: The Settling of the North American Continent* (New York: Simon & Schuster, 1993), p. 113.

2. Ibid., p. 112.

3. Price, David A., *Love and Hate in Jamestown* (New York: Alfred A. Knopf, 2003), p. 52.

4. Morgan, p. 114.

5. Niles, Blair, *The James* (New York: Farrar & Rinehart, 1939), p. 31.

Chapter 5
Things Get Worse, Then Better

1. Price, David A., *Love and Hate in Jamestown* (New York: Alfred A. Knopf, 2003), p. 173.

2. Morgan, Ted, *Wilderness at Dawn: The Settling of the North American Continent* (New York: Simon & Schuster, 1993), p. 129.

Chronology

1606	James I awards charter to investors, calling their company The Virginia Company of London
December 19	Captain Newport's three ships, the *Susan Constant*, the *Godspeed*, and the *Discovery* leave England for Virginia
1607	
April 26	The Jamestown fleet sails into the Chesapeake Bay
May 13	Fort James is established
May 27	Men begin work on fortifying the fort by building a triangular wooden wall around the encampment
June 10	John Smith is released from arrest and sworn in as a member of the council
June 22	Captain Newport leaves Fort James for England
September 10	President Wingfield is removed and Ratcliff is elected
December	John Smith is captured by Powhatans
December 30	John Smith meets the great chief Powhatan

Chronology (cont'd)

1608

Early January	Powhatan releases Smith; Captain Newport returns to Fort James with 100 new settlers to find only 38 survivors
January 7	Fire destroys most of the fort
April 10	Captain Newport returns to England
September 10	Smith is elected President
	Captain Newport returns with the colony's first women

1609

May 23	The Virginia Company in England decides to replace the council with a governor who has absolute rule
August	Seven ships arrive at Fort James, minus the *Sea Venture*, which is thought to be lost at sea
September	Captain George Percy replaces John Smith as president of the council
October	Smith returns to England
	Captain John Ratcliffe is tortured to death

1610 — Acting governor Thomas Gates decides to abandon the fort after arriving early in May to find 60 emaciated colonists

Governor De La Warr arrives in Virginia soon after Gates and orders everyone back to the fort

1611 — Governor De La Warr returns to England in March, leaving George Percy in charge of the 150 settlers as Deputy Governor

May 12	Governor Thomas Dale arrives
August	Sir Thomas Gates returns with 280 settlers and assumes control
	Thomas Dale takes 350 men and moves to Henrico

1612 John Rolfe exports the colony's first crop of good tobacco to England

1613 Pocahontas is kidnapped and brought to Jamestown

1614 John Rolfe and Pocahontas are married on April 5

1616 Governor George Yeardley replaces Dale; the Rolfes leave Virginia for England

1617 Pocahontas dies in England on March 21 at the age of 21

1618 Powhatan dies in spring; headright system established

1619 First meeting of the Virginia House of Burgesses

1622 Powhatans kill 347 settlers on March 22

1623 After negotiating peace with a Powhatan village, Captain William Tucker proposes a toast with a poisonous drink; 200 Indians die from the poison, and 50 more are slaughtered

1624 James I revokes the company charter and takes over Virginia as a royal colony on May 24

1651 First Indian Reservation is established for Powhatan Indians

1699 The General Assembly moves Virginia's capital to Williamsburg (Middle Plantation)

Timeline in History

1506	Christopher Columbus dies at the age of 55.
1558	Elizabeth I is crowned Queen of England and Ireland.
1562	Jean Ribault establishes Huguenot colony at Port Royal, South Carolina (also called Charles Fort).
1563	The Huguenots abandon Port Royal.
1565	The Spanish establish St. Augustine in Florida.
1572	Francis Drake embarks on his first expedition as a privateer.
1580	Sir Francis Drake returns from his famous voyage around the world.
1585	Sir Walter Raleigh sponsors a voyage to Roanoke Island.
1587	John White, sent by Sir Walter Raleigh, establishes Roanoke Island colony. Virginia Dare, John White's granddaughter, is born in Roanoke on August 18—she is the first white child born in North America.
1590	John White returns to Roanoke Island to find the colony completely empty.
1592	Captain Christopher Newport captures a Spanish ship in the West Indies.
1602	Captains Bartholomew Gosnold, Bartholomew Gilbert, and Gabriel Archer scout the coast of New England.
1603	James VI of Scotland succeeds Elizabeth I as King James I of England.
1610	Henry Hudson finds Hudson Bay; the French found Quebec.
1611	King James Version of the Bible is published.
1618	Sir Walter Raleigh is executed.
1620	The *Mayflower* pilgrims land at Plymouth, New England.
1625	Charles I becomes King of England.
1642	England revolts against Charles I.
1649	Charles I is executed.
1655	Oliver Cromwell dissolves English Parliament.
1658	Oliver Cromwell dies.
1660	Charles II becomes King.
1664	The English take New York.

Further Reading

For Young Adults

Adams, Patricia. *The Story of Pocahontas: Indian Princess.* Milwaukee: Gareth Stevens Publishing, 1987.

Fishwick, Marshall W. *Jamestown: First English Colony.* New York: American Heritage Publishing Co., Inc., 1965.

Fritz, Jean. *The Double Life of Pocahontas.* New York: Putnam, 1983.

Neal, Harry Edward. *The Virginia Colony.* New York: Hawthorn Books, Inc. 1969.

Stiles, Martha Bennett. *One Among the Indians.* New York: The Dial Press, 1962.

Works Consulted

Niles, Blair. *The James.* New York: Farrar & Rinehart, 1939.

Dowdey, Clifford. *The Virginia Dynasties.* New York: Little, Brown, and Company, 1969.

Morgan, Ted. *Wilderness at Dawn: The Settling of the North American Continent.* New York: Simon & Schuster, 1993.

Price, David A. *Love and Hate in Jamestown.* New York: Alfred A. Knopf, 2003.

On the Internet

Jamestown 1607: Windows to the New World
http://www.jamestown1607.org/

Jamestown Rediscovery
http://www.apva.org/jr.html

Historic Jamestowne
http://www.historicjamestowne.org/

Settler's Instructions
http://jamestown2007.org/jamestownadventure/instructions_q1.html

Jamestown 2007
http://jamestown2007.org

Virtual Jamestown: "Powhatan"
http://www.virtualjamestown.org/Powhat1.html

Glossary

adversaries
(AD-ver-sayr-eez)
Opponents or enemies.

alliance
(uh-LIE-uns)
A close association, formed to advance common interests or causes.

apprentice
(uh-PREN-tus)
One bound by legal agreement to work for another for a specific amount of time in return for instruction in a trade, art, or business.

brackish
(BRAA-kish)
Having a small amount of salt or salt water.

clapboard
(KLAH-berd)
Long narrow boards with one edge thicker than the other; these are overlapped horizontally to cover outer walls.

coerce
(ko-ERS)
To force someone to act or think in a certain way by use of pressure, threats, or intimidation.

defuse
(dee-FYOOZ)
To make less dangerous or tense.

dehydrate
(dee-HY-drayt)
To lose water.

incarcerate
(in-KAR-seh-rayt)
To put in jail or confine as punishment.

indentured servitude
(in-DEN-churd SER-vih-tood)
Owing several years of work to repay money or ownership of land.

indict
(in-DYT)
To accuse of wrongdoing.

lethargic
(leh-THAR-jik)
Lacking energy because of disease or injury.

munitions
(myoo-NIH-shens)
Weapons and ammunition.

nemesis
(NEH-meh-sis)
An opponent or rival.

privateer
(pry-veh-TEER)
A captain who owns a ship and is authorized by a government to attack and capture enemy vessels during war.

protocol
(PRO-tuh-kall)
A code of correct conduct.

pyrite
(PY-ryt)
A commonly occurring iron-based mineral that is often mistaken for gold; also called fool's gold.

ruse
(ROOZ)
A cunning trick.

savages
(SAA-vih-jes)
An uncivilized people, usually living in harsh and isolated conditions. The English settlers considered the Native Americans to be uncivilized.

scrutiny
(SKROOT-nee)
A careful examination.

sedition
(seh-DIH-shun)
The inciting of others to rebel or commit treason.

shallop
(SHAH-lup)
A small open boat used to navigate shallow waters.

wanderlust
(WAN-der-lust)
An irresistible urge to travel.

Index

Anne, Queen   38

Argall, Samuel   37

Bacon, Nathaniel   40–41

Berkeley, Sir William   40–41

Cassen, George   22

Charles I, King   40

Chesapeake Bay   8, 10, 13, 23, 26, 33, 37, 40

Chickahominy River   21, 23

Cromwell, Oliver   40

Dale's Gift   37

Dale, Thomas   37

De La Warr, Lord   32, 36, 37

Discovery   7, 8, 18, 30

Elizabeth I, Queen   11

Gates, Thomas   32, 36

Glorious Revolution   41

Godspeed   7, 8

Gosnold, Bartholomew   7, 8, 13

Great Rebellion   40

Headright program   38

Henrico   37

House of Burgesses   40

Hunt, Robert   8, 18

James I, King   11, 14, 40

James II, King   41

James River   10, 14, 15, 23, 36, 39, 40, 41

James River Falls   10

Japazeus   37

Kecoughtan   37

King Charles   40

London   7, 32

Martin, John   13

Matoaka *see* Pocahontas

Middle Plantation *see* Williamsburg

Newport, Christopher   7, 13, 14, 16, 19, 21, 25, 26, 29, 34

Nonpareil *see* Pocahontas

Opechancanough   22

Pacific Ocean   11, 13, 14

Paspahegh   10, 17, 18

Patawomeck   37

Percy, George   9–10, 18, 32, 35, 36

Pocahontas   24, 25, 26, 27, 30, 31, 32, 33, 37, 38, 40, 42

Potomac River   37

Powhatan
  chief   15, 22, 24, 26, 27, 29, 30, 31, 34, 35, 36, 37, 39
  people   15, 16, 21, 22, 23, 24, 25, 26, 27, 30, 31, 32, 33, 35, 36, 37, 38, 39, 40, 41

Raleigh, Sir Walter   11

Ratcliffe, John   7, 8, 13, 21, 25, 26, 35, 36

Roanoke Island   11

Rolfe, John   33, 37, 40, 42

Rolfe, Rebecca *see* Pocahontas

Sea Venture   32, 36, 42

Smith, John   8, 10, 13, 14, 16, 17, 19, 21, 22, 24, 25, 26, 27, 29, 30, 3, 32, 33, 35, 36, 3

Spanish   7, 13, 14, 21, 33

Starving Time   36

Susan Constant   7, 10, 13

swamp fever   26

tobacco   37, 39, 40, 42

Virginia   7, 9, 10, 11, 12, 14, 15, 17, 27, 28, 32, 33, 36, 38, 39, 40, 41

Virginia Company of London   7, 11, 33

Williamsburg   23, 41

Wingfield, Edward-Maria   13, 14, 16, 17, 18, 19

Wyatt, Sir Francis   39

Yeardley, George   37, 38

York River   15, 23